Lost in the Labyrinth

by L. A. Peacock

Scholastic Inc.
New York Toronto London Auckland
Sydney Mexico City New Delhi Hong Kong

To Jessica Dube and Joshua Yarro,
with love — L.A.F.

ISBN 978-0-545-24765-8

12 11 10 9 8 7 6 5 4 3 2 10 11 12 13 14 15/0

Printed in the U.S.A. 40

First Scholastic printing, September 2010

Chapter 1

Up in the Attic

"Jessica! Joshua!" A loud voice called from inside their big house.

Jess sat on the porch. The Book Wizard was in her hand. Jess liked to read electronic books on the Wizard. She looked up lots of cool facts on the Wizard's encyclopedia, too.

Their mother called again.

"Okay, we're coming!" shouted Jess. She finished reading the page, then turned off the Wizard.

Jess stood up and looked around for her brother. Where was Josh now?

The street was quiet. Tall oak trees were on each side. Josh was riding his new skateboard.

Jess waved her arms.

"Josh! Hurry up!" shouted Jess. "Mom's calling us."

"Now what?" Josh groaned.

He kicked up the board and walked toward the house. It was big, just like their old house in Chicago. The Baxter family had just moved back to Boston. Jess and Josh's father was going to start his new teaching job at the college the next week.

Jess was waiting in the doorway.

"Are you coming, slowpoke?" Jess made a silly face.

Oh, brother, Josh thought. His sister was a real pain.

Jess liked to boss around her ten-year-old twin brother. Josh was bigger and two minutes older. But that didn't matter to Jess.

"Mom and Dad are unpacking the boxes the movers left," said Jess. "We promised Mom we'd put away our own stuff."

MOV

Jess tucked the Wizard into her sweatshirt. Josh was good with computers, too, but he mostly played video games. He liked *real* games, too. Football and basketball were his best sports.

"Oh, man," said Josh. "Let's unpack our stuff later." He wanted to stay outside and practice new tricks on his skateboard.

"Come on," Jess said. "Meet you upstairs." She turned and ran into the front hall.

Great-grandfather Baxter had built the Boston house years before. Now it belonged to the twins' dad and Uncle Harry, a famous explorer. Harry had disappeared on his last trip, four years earlier. Their parents were worried. Uncle Harry was lost, maybe dead.

"Hey, Jess," yelled Josh, "where are you?"

Josh found his sister on the third floor.

"In here!" Jess called from the back bedroom. Boxes and suitcases were open everywhere. Jess had tons of books. And clothes!

Ugh, thought Josh. Why did girls need so much stuff? He carried his two boxes into his room. It took Josh only ten minutes to put away his things.

An hour later, Jess was standing in Josh's doorway.

"Mom wants the suitcases in the attic," said Jess. "Come with me."

Josh laughed. "What, are you afraid of ghosts?" His sister read a lot of mysteries.

"Me, afraid of ghosts? No way!" said Jess.

Josh reached across the bed and grabbed his flashlight. He handed it to Jess.

"Take it," said Josh. "Call me if you see a ghost."

Jess folded her arms.

"That's funny, Josh. Get up and help me," Jess ordered. "Or I'll call Mom." The attic was dark and spooky. Maybe she was just a little afraid.

"Okay, okay. You win." Josh put down his video game.

They walked to the end of the hall. Hanging from the ceiling was a rope. Josh pulled. A wooden ladder dropped down.

Josh handed the flashlight to Jess. He took the suitcases and climbed up the ladder.

Jess switched on the flashlight. She pointed the beam of light at the ceiling door. Then at the lock.

The bolt slid easily. Josh put his shoulder against the ceiling door and pushed it open.

He crawled into the dark attic.

Two small windows let in some light. The air was stale and musty. The attic was filled with strange shapes.

Slowly, Jess followed her brother up the ladder.

"It sure is creepy in here," whispered Jess. Maybe there *were* ghosts in the attic. After all,

Uncle Harry was probably dead. And this was his house.

The light from the flashlight made dark shadows against the walls. There were some old furniture, dozens of boxes, and all kinds of stuff.

Jess held the beam of light still. A big trunk was in the corner.

"I wonder what's in *that*," Josh said. He walked over to get a better look.

Jess heard a rustling sound. She turned around.

"What was that noise?" she whispered. *Maybe it was a ghost!*

A small furry creature peeked from behind the trunk. It ran across the floor.

Jess screamed, jumping out of the way.

"What?" Josh looked up.

Jess pointed to the trunk. "I saw something. It came from over there!"

"Don't be a scaredy-cat," said Josh. "It's just a squirrel." Behind the trunk, he found a nest with some nuts and berries in it.

"Let's move this trunk next to a window," said Josh. "I bet it belongs to Uncle Harry."

The trunk was covered with dust.

"Yuck!" said Jess. She was wearing her favorite pink sweatshirt.

Jess went over to the trunk. Carefully, she grabbed the leather handle on the front and pulled.

"Boy, is this thing dirty. And *heavy*!" Jess groaned.

Josh's sister complained a lot.

"Just pull it," Josh said. He pushed hard from behind.

They moved the trunk slowly, inch by inch, into the light.

"Look at all the cool stickers," said Josh. "See the ones on top? They're from Egypt, Greece, Italy, Mexico, India, Africa, Peru . . ."

Jess counted more than twenty stickers. Uncle Harry had traveled all over the world.

"That lock is really old." Jess pointed to the rusty bolt on the front of the trunk.

Josh tried to move the bolt, but it was stuck. He looked around the attic for a tool.

He had an idea.

"Hand me the flashlight," Josh said.

Josh took the flashlight from Jess and banged it hard against the bolt.

"It's not a hammer," warned Jess. "Don't break it!" Her brother always had ideas. And they usually got the twins into trouble.

After a few taps, the old lock snapped open.

"See? No problem." Josh smiled. He raised the lid of the trunk. It made a funny, creaky sound. Dust was flying everywhere.

Josh stuck his head inside the trunk.

"It's dark. I can't see much," he muttered.

Jess pointed the beam of light inside the

trunk. A cardboard box was on top. A few pictures were sticking out of it.

"This is spooky," Jess whispered. "Look at those old photographs."

Josh picked up a photo of a young man. "I bet that's Uncle Harry," he said. The man had a leather bag on his shoulder. A brown leather hat was pulled over his eyes. A shovel was in his hand.

"Hey, he looks like Dad and *you*!" Jess said. All the Baxter men were tall and thin. They had brown wavy hair and thin noses.

"Yeah, but we don't have long hair!" said Josh. Uncle Harry's hair was tied back into a ponytail.

There were more photographs. Josh found a cool one of an old temple and a bunch of stone statues. He handed the photo to Jess.

"I bet Uncle Harry was in Greece," she said. "We studied Greek myths last year, remember? What else is in the trunk?"

Josh pulled out a thick book with a leather cover and flipped through it. It was filled with lots of writing, drawings, and old maps. There were dates at the tops of the pages.

"What's that?" asked Jess. "It looks like a journal."

Josh turned to the first page. He looked at the signature.

"Right. It belongs to Uncle Harry." Josh turned the pages slowly. He found a map.

"Uncle Harry was looking for something in

Greece. Check out this map," Josh said.

Jess moved closer. An arrow pointed to a large island southeast of Athens. It was called Crete.

"Look at the top of the page," said Josh. "At the date."

Jess stared at the journal. "What? That can't be right," she whispered.

"Uncle Harry wrote in this journal a *month* ago!" said Josh, shaking his head.

Jess was confused. How was this possible?

"Do you think Uncle Harry was *here*?" she asked. "Is he still alive?"

Josh nodded. "But where is he *now*?"

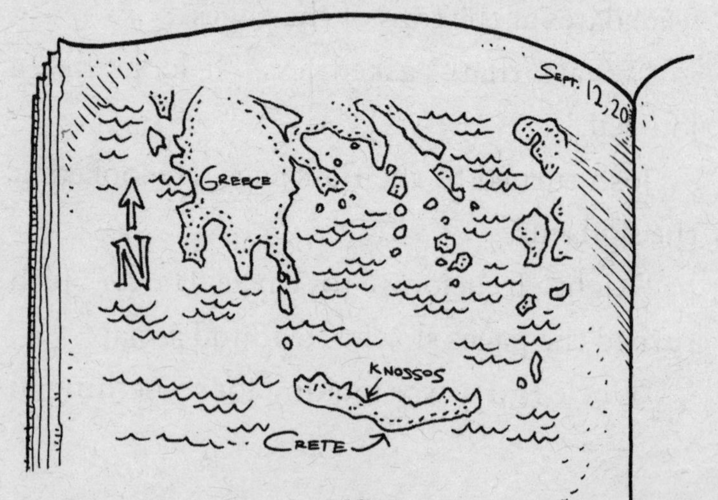

Chapter 2

The Magic Trunk

"What should we do?" asked Jess. *Was there a ghost in the attic?*

Josh gazed at the journal. Why was it in the trunk? Who put it there, and why?

"Uncle Harry needs our help," Josh said. "He wants us to find him." That was the only explanation.

"No way!" Jess turned to go down the stairs. "I'm telling Mom and Dad," she said.

"Wait. Don't be such a baby," Josh said. He wasn't ready to give up. "I bet this map can help us."

Jess stared at her brother. Maybe Josh was

right. Was it a magic trunk? Was Uncle Harry still alive?

"Okay. Show me," she said. Jess crouched down next to Josh.

Josh pointed to the map of Crete. "See this ancient city? It's called . . . K-nos-sos . . . or . . . something like that. I bet that's where Uncle Harry is now."

"You're crazy," Jess said. "How can he go back and forth in time?"

Josh shook his head.

"I don't know how. But I think he can," said Josh. "Uncle Harry came back last month. He left his journal in the trunk. What else could it be?"

Jess looked at the map. *Follow the clues,* she thought. Just like they did in the mystery stories in her books.

She took the Wizard out of her pocket. The menu screen lit up. She clicked on the encyclopedia.

Jess typed in G-R-E-E-C-E, then C-R-E-T-E.

"Spell the name of that city," said Jess.

Josh frowned. Jess was bossy, all right. But she was smart, too.

"It's K-n-o-s-s-o-s." Josh spelled the name slowly.

Jess typed the letters into the Wizard. She clicked Search and read out loud:

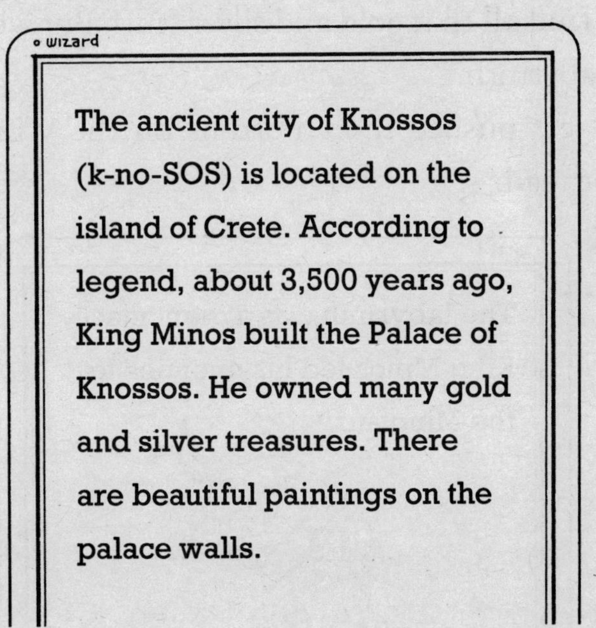

"Wait, there's more," said Jess. She read on:

> wizard
>
> **King Minos built the labyrinth to hide the Minotaur. This monster had the body of a man and the head of a bull.**

"Cool," said Josh. "I bet Uncle Harry wanted to find all that gold and silver stuff. But what's a labyrinth?"

Jess pushed more buttons on the Wizard. She read:

"Gross!" said Jess. "Take a look. The Minotaur is pretty ugly." The picture on the screen showed a beast that was half man, half bull.

"The Minotaur is a myth," Jess said. "We don't know if it's a true story or not. It happened a long time ago."

"I wish I could see a real Minotaur!" Josh said. Video games with monsters and aliens were his favorites.

"Forget it," warned Jess. "Let's get Mom and Dad. They'll know what to do."

Jess turned around. She headed for the stairs again.

Josh grabbed her arm, stopping her. "No, wait!" he said. "Uncle Harry wants *us* to help him. I just know it."

Jess sighed. Maybe Josh was right. Josh and Jess were a team.

"Okay. I won't tell," she said.

Jess turned off the Wizard and grabbed the flashlight.

"Maybe Uncle Harry left another clue," she said. Josh got on his knees and searched the trunk. Jess held the flashlight.

"Do you see anything?" she asked.

"Just some old clothes," Josh said. "Wait, I can feel a bag."

Josh held up a brown bag. It was made of leather and had a thick strap.

"It's like the one in the photo. That bag belongs to Uncle Harry," said Jess.

Josh reached into the bag. He felt a flat, round thing. It was made of metal.

"Hey, there's something in here," said Josh. "And it's heavy."

"Let me see," said Jess. Maybe it was an ancient treasure.

Josh pulled the thing out slowly.

"What's *that*?" Jess asked. It looked golden in the light. And old.

Josh looked more closely. "It looks like a clock. See the twelve marks, like numbers?

It has hands like a clock, too." He turned the thing around. He wasn't sure *what* it was.

"Give it to me." Jess pointed the beam of light on the strange object.

Josh handed it over. "Be careful. Don't drop it."

"I think it's a compass, too," said Jess. The flashlight lit the letters *N*, *S*, *E*, and *W*. Jess read them out loud. "That means north, south, east, and west."

Josh turned the bag upside down. A small piece of stone fell out.

Jess put down the compass, picked up the stone, and turned it over in her hand. A line of pictures was carved into the stone.

"Hey, they look like the marks on the time-compass thing," said Josh. "Maybe they're numbers."

"I don't know," said Jess. Maybe Uncle Harry had left more clues in the journal.

Jess flipped through the pages. She found something.

"Look at this stone tablet." Jess pointed to a drawing of a stone tablet in Uncle Harry's journal. It was from an ancient temple.

Josh took a closer look. "Hey, there's a piece missing."

"I think I know where it is," said Jess. "Right here!" She held out the piece of stone.

Josh picked up the stone and looked at the marks. Then he picked up the time-compass. He looked from one to the other. They were the same marks!

"I know what you're thinking," said Jess. She was shaking her head.

Josh started moving three hands around the time-compass. He was matching the marks on the time-compass with the marks on the stone.

"Don't, Josh!" warned Jess. "I have a bad feeling about this!"

Josh was lining up the numbers.

The hands on the time-compass were making clicking sounds.

The thing was working!

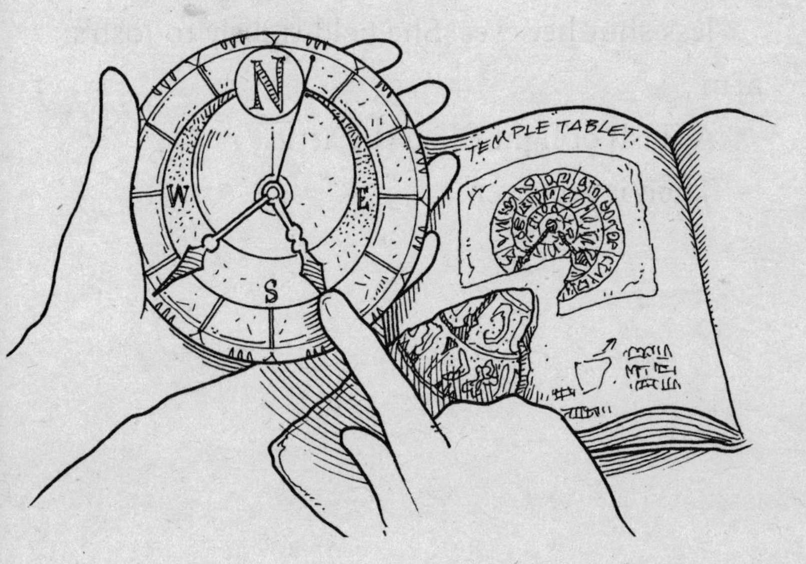

"Oh, no!" shouted Jess.

Josh grabbed the journal, the stone, and Uncle Harry's bag.

"Get ready!" he shouted.

Jess felt the pocket of her sweatshirt. The Wizard was still there.

Click! Click! Click! Josh matched the last three marks on the time-compass.

The room was shaking. The floor was moving round and round.

Jess shut her eyes. She held tightly to Josh's arm.

A flash of light filled the attic.

Then it was over.

Chapter 3

A New Friend

Jess opened her eyes slowly. She looked around.

The sun was hot. The air was dry and filled with dust.

Josh was staring at the time-compass in his hand. Uncle Harry's leather bag was over his shoulder.

"Oh, no!" said Jess. "Where are we?"

The wind was blowing through the trees. But these trees were different. Not like the ones at home.

Then Jess looked down.

"And what happened to our clothes?" She felt the long dress. It was all white, and soft, like her bathrobe. It was magic!

Jess laughed when she saw her brother.

"Look at you! How do you like wearing a *dress*?"

Josh's T-shirt and jeans were gone. He was wearing a white tunic with a leather belt. His long legs were bare under the short skirt. The sandals on his feet were tied around his ankles.

"This is so weird," he said. "Where are my sneakers? How do you run in these things?" Josh moved his feet up and down.

"I like these clothes," said Jess, twirling around on her new leather sandals. She found a pocket in her robe. The Book Wizard was there.

Josh walked over to a funny-looking tree. He plucked some olives. "I think we're in Crete. The time-compass works, all right."

"Oh, great," said Jess. "I hope it can get us back home."

But first they had to find Uncle Harry.

They heard a strange braying sound.

"Donkeys," said Josh. He pointed at the fields behind the olive trees. A man was filling baskets with olives. Two boys loaded the baskets onto a wooden wagon.

Jess and Josh watched the younger boy. He hitched the donkey to the wagon. Then he climbed up onto the wagon and grabbed the reins.

Right in front of them was a road. Josh saw a city in the distance.

Josh turned to Jess. He had a plan.

"Come on," he said. "Let's follow that wagon."

Jess shaded her eyes from the bright sun. The city looked far away. There were steep hills ahead.

"Hey, you don't expect me to walk all that way in these sandals?" complained Jess. She ran after her brother.

“Man, I wish I had my skateboard,” said Josh. “These hills are perfect for tricks.”

The wagon was pulling into the road. The boy tugged on the reins until the donkey stopped. He was waving and calling out to Jess and Josh.

“Huh? I wonder what he wants,” said Josh.

“Maybe he wants to give us a ride,” said Jess. Her feet hurt.

Jess smiled at the boy. She waved back.

“I think he likes you,” Josh said. “You look pretty cute in that dress.”

“And so do you.” Jess laughed.

Chapter 4

On the Road to Knossos

Jess and Josh ran over to the wagon. The boy reached out and helped Jess up. She sat in the seat behind him.

"Thanks," she said, and smiled again. The boy was dressed like Josh. His hair was dark and curly. A gold bracelet with a snake design was on his right arm.

Josh climbed up. He threw the leather bag under the seat and sat next to the boy.

The wagon moved slowly. More and more people were on the road now.

"Are you from Athens?" asked the boy in his ancient language. He turned to look at Jess. "My name is Icarus."

Jess stared at Josh. She understood the boy's language! It was more magic from the time-compass.

"I'm Jess, and this is my brother, Josh," she said in ancient Greek. She made the new sounds easily.

"We're just . . . er . . . visiting." Josh could speak the strange language, too.

"Yeah, our uncle," said Jess. "We're not sure where he lives." She pointed to the city ahead.

"Ah, Knossos. That's where I live," said Icarus. "At the palace, with my father. That was our farm back there."

Suddenly, Icarus pulled back on the reins. Bigger wagons were crossing the road ahead of them. Dozens of clay jars were tied together in the backs of some. Other wagons carried baskets of grain and olives.

They were getting closer to the city gate. A high stone wall surrounded the buildings.

Jess slipped her hand into her robe pocket.

She pulled out the Wizard. She clicked on its encyclopedia and entered P-A-L-A-C-E O-F K-N-O-S-S-O-S. She read:

o wizard

Visitors enter the palace from the west gate. The great staircase leads to the central court and throne room.

"Is that the west gate?" asked Jess. She pointed to an opening in the wall.

Icarus nodded. "Yes. That's the best way to the palace."

Jess turned to Josh and whispered into his ear, "Maybe Uncle Harry is in the palace. That's where King Minos keeps his treasures."

Icarus moved the wagon to the side. A group of soldiers marched by. Some men in short tunics followed them. Banners were flying in the wind.

The people on the road were cheering.

"Those athletes are the champion bull riders," said Icarus.

Jess looked up. She made a face.

"Ugh, bulls! How do you ride bulls?"

Icarus laughed. "It's a contest. Whoever leaps highest over the bull wins."

"Wow, I'd like to see that!" said Josh.

"The contests start this afternoon at the palace," said Icarus.

He turned around.

"Do *you* want to go, Jess?" asked Icarus. "Girls are in the contest, too. The girls dance in front of the bulls, and the boys leap over."

Jess didn't like that idea at all. She wanted to find Uncle Harry and go home.

Josh answered for her. "Sure she does. Jess isn't afraid of anything."

A big smile spread across Josh's face. Jess wouldn't back down now.

Jess stared at Josh. She didn't smile this time.

"Oh, all right," she said. "But first we have to find our uncle Harry."

"I can ask my father," Icarus said. "He built the labyrinth for King Minos. He knows everyone at the palace."

"Hey, isn't the labyrinth that super maze?" Josh asked.

Jess was worried. She remembered what the Wizard had said.

"Icarus," she asked, "is it true, you know, about the Minotaur?"

"Yeah," Josh said. "Is there *really* a man-eating monster? Does he hide in the labyrinth?"

Icarus nodded. He turned to Jess and Josh.

"The Minotaur protects the palace," he whispered softly. "If the guards capture a thief, they throw the thief in the labyrinth. That's how they feed the Minotaur."

Josh knew one thing for sure.

They needed to find Uncle Harry . . . and fast.

Chapter 5

The Palace

"Let's go that way," said Josh. The bull riders were marching through the west gate.

Josh threw the leather bag over his shoulder and climbed down from the wagon. Jess was already on the ground.

"Follow them to the palace," said Icarus. "The athletes are going to the central court."

Beyond the walls were white stone buildings with wooden columns and roofs. Men were pushing carts of vegetables along the rough stone paths. Women and children carried sacks of grain. It was a busy day in the city.

"Thanks for the ride," said Jess. She waved good-bye to their new friend.

"I'll find you at the contest," shouted Icarus. He turned the wagon and disappeared in the crowd.

"Now what?" asked Jess. Crowds of people were blocking the road.

"I have a bad feeling," she said. "Maybe we should go home now!"

Josh looked in the leather bag. The time-compass was still there. So were the journal and the piece of stone tablet with the funny picture writing.

"But how?" he asked, shaking his head. "We need Uncle Harry to help us."

Jess looked up. Ahead was the great Palace of Knossos.

"Come on," she shouted, pointing to the palace. "Let's look for clues."

"Yeah, and Uncle Harry, too," said Josh.

Josh grabbed Jess's hand and ran to the side entrance. "Hurry, Jess," he whispered, "before anyone catches us."

The twins ducked into an open doorway.

They walked slowly down a dark passageway. An open area was just ahead. Storerooms were on each side. Huge jars of olive oil and wine were tied to wooden platforms. Baskets of grain were lined up against the walls.

Big pieces of meat hung from iron hooks. Kitchen workers were lighting fires under iron pots. Bakers were taking bread out of the large ovens.

Jess and Josh hid behind a storage basket.

"King Minos must be having a party," whispered Jess. "People talk at parties. That's a good place to look for clues about Uncle Harry."

Some servants were pouring wine into clay jugs.

Josh had an idea. He reached out and grabbed a metal tray with two pretty silver cups on it.

"Hide these in your pocket," Josh said, handing the cups and tray to Jess.

"Are you nuts?" asked Jess. She knew what happened to thieves!

"Don't worry," said Josh. "We'll need them later." He slipped a small jug of wine into the leather bag. It just fit.

Jess stopped next to a large wooden door. She reached into her pocket and pulled out the Wizard.

"We'd better check the palace floor plan." Jess typed in some words and clicked Search. She looked closely at the map and found the kitchen area.

"Okay, what direction?" asked Josh. "What should we look for?"

"The grand staircase," Jess said. She looked around for a flight of stairs.

"Over there," she said, pointing to the right. "The throne room is four flights up."

The stairs were narrow and dark. Slowly, Josh led Jess up the flat stones to the top.

Double doors opened into a large room.

They walked in.

"Look at this!" Josh said. Colorful paintings filled the walls. There were dozens of dolphins, all shapes and sizes. The wooden columns along the sides were painted in bright colors, too.

Jess stood in the middle of the room and twirled. "Wow! It looks like the aquarium at home."

Josh shook his head. "I don't think they had aquariums in ancient Crete."

Suddenly, loud voices came from the hall.

People were coming. It was too late to hide.

Quickly, Josh pulled out the tray.

Jess grabbed the tray from Josh. She took the silver cups from her pocket. Josh held the jug of wine.

The twins looked like servants.

The doors opened. Two guards stood in front of Jess and Josh. They looked angry.

"There you are," said the taller guard. "Hurry, the king is thirsty."

Jess and Josh nodded. The guards led them down another hallway. Jess held the tray high. Her hands were shaking.

They stepped into a large noisy room. It was filled with people in white robes. The women were wearing gold and silver jewelry. At the end of the room, a small man was sitting on a white stone chair on a platform.

"This must be the throne room," Jess said softly.

“And that must be King Minos,” whispered Josh.

A guard took the tray and cups from Jess. Josh handed him the wine. People were talking about the bull-riding contest, not about Uncle Harry. The guards moved around the king. He was getting ready to leave.

“Quick, let’s get out of here!” said Josh. “Do you know the way out?”

Jess glanced down at the Wizard. The palace plan was still on the screen.

“I think the central courtyard is that way,” she said. Jess pointed to some double doors on the north side of the room.

No one was looking. All eyes were on the king.

“Now!” whispered Josh. He moved backward one step at a time.

Slowly, Jess followed.

No one saw them leave.

They turned and ran. Another dark,

winding hallway was just ahead. They hurried down the staircase.

"Are you sure this is the way to the central courtyard?" asked Josh.

Jess stopped next to an open window. Another colorful painting was on the wall. She found the same painting on the Wizard.

Josh and Jess stared at the painting. It was of two girl dancers and a bull. A boy was leaping onto the bull's back.

"Oh, boy!" said Josh. "Icarus wasn't kidding. Those guys really do ride bulls! Girls help, too. One girl runs in front of the bull."

"It looks dangerous," said Jess.

"No, it's fun!" Josh said. "It's like gymnastics. Or like a flip on a skateboard!"

Josh looked more closely at the picture. He tried to figure out the trick.

"First you dive over the horns, then twist backward. You need to push off with your hands on the bull's back," said Josh. "I think that's how they do it."

"Don't get any ideas," warned Jess. She knew her brother. Josh liked a dare.

A trumpet sounded outside the window.

"Come on. The contest is starting. We have to find Icarus," she said, racing out the door.

Josh ran after Jess. Suddenly, he stopped and glanced back. Josh took a last look at the picture of the bull rider.

A big smile was on Josh's face.

"Piece of cake!" he said under his breath.

Chapter 6

The Bull Pen

The sun was high in the sky. The contest was about to begin.

The crowd was filling the benches along the sides of the courtyard. A large open space was in the middle.

Near the entrance was a boxed area with a platform. Wooden columns held up a tent of golden cloth. Under the tent were two large chairs made of white stone. The chairs were decorated with gold and jewels. The thrones were empty.

"I bet those chairs are for King Minos and the queen," said Jess.

A small crowd gathered behind the benches

on the right side. Josh and Jess looked around. Icarus wasn't there.

"Maybe Icarus is at the bull pens," said Josh. He pointed to the practice area.

Jess looked across the open courtyard. Some people were watching the bulls.

"Yuck!" cried Jess. "Do we have to go there?" It was a hot day. The smell from the bull pens was strong. Jess pinched her nose and followed Josh.

They moved through the crowd slowly. At last, they stood in front of the pen with the largest bull.

"Wow, look at that big one," Josh said. "He looks really mean!"

He was the biggest animal Jess had ever seen. The bull's horns were long and sharp. A large metal ring was in his nose.

"I wonder who's going to ride *him,*" Josh said. Around the pen, the young bull riders were yelling and throwing sticks at the bull.

“He’s a monster!” said Jess.

The bull’s head was down. He was snorting loudly and stomping his feet.

Some bull riders were stretching and jumping next to the pens. Their jumps were high. But Josh knew he could leap just as high.

Josh felt a tap on his shoulder. He turned around.

Icarus was standing behind them.

“You found us!” Josh said. “Isn’t this cool, Icarus?” He pointed to the bull pen.

Icarus looked worried.

“What’s wrong?” asked Jess.

“Did you find our uncle Harry?” Josh asked.

“No,” said Icarus. “But my father told me about a thief. The man took some treasure from the palace. His name is Ah-ri. He must be your uncle.”

Jess stood back. “Uncle Harry is an explorer,” she said. “He’s *not* a thief!”

"I believe you," said Icarus, "but King Minos is angry. The palace guards took your uncle to the labyrinth."

Icarus pulled his friends away from the crowd. He picked up a stick and started to draw in the dirt.

Jess and Josh moved closer to get a better look. It was a sketch of a giant maze.

"Is that the labyrinth?" asked Jess. "The maze your father built?"

"Yes," said Icarus. "Your uncle is here, in the guardhouse." He pointed to the middle of the labyrinth.

Josh took the stick and traced the winding passages. He stopped at the top of the maze.

"Is that where they keep the . . . the Minotaur?" Jess choked on the word.

Icarus nodded. "After the bull-riding contest, they will feed the Minotaur."

Josh took Uncle Harry's journal from the leather bag. Quickly, he copied the drawing of the labyrinth.

"Is there a way out of the maze, Icarus?" asked Jess.

"There is a hidden gate," Icarus said. "My father showed me. Here."

He pointed the stick at one of the passages on the far wall.

Josh marked the spot of the secret gate in the journal. It wasn't far from the guardhouse.

"We need to find Uncle Harry," said Josh, closing the journal.

"And rescue him," said Jess.

"Before it's too late!"

Chapter 7

The Bull-Riding Contest

The trumpet sounded again. This time it was much louder.

People started to leave the pens. They moved into the benches around the open court.

Icarus looked up. The king and queen were taking their seats in the golden tent.

"King Minos has arrived," Icarus said. "The contests are starting soon."

Josh glanced back at the bulls. He had an idea.

"Icarus," asked Josh, "can you get me and Jess into the contest? Maybe the king will help us if we win."

"No way!" Jess cried. She wanted to help,

but this time Josh had gone too far.

"Come on, Jess," Josh pleaded. "You can do it. Wave your hands and get the bull to chase you. I'll ride the bull."

Jess was afraid. She turned to Icarus.

"Will the king really free Uncle Harry if we win?" she asked.

Icarus nodded. "Josh is right," he said. "The king might listen if you win the bull-riding contest."

"This is the worst plan you've ever had, Josh," said Jess, shaking her head. But they had to help Uncle Harry. And get back home.

Jess took a deep breath. "Okay, I'll do it."

Icarus walked over to the pen where the athletes were standing. He pointed to Jess and Josh. Then he called them over.

"These are my friends from Athens," said Icarus. "My money says they can win the contest."

The athletes laughed. Josh didn't look like

much of a bull rider. Jess looked scared.

A young bull rider stepped up to Josh. “So, you think you can ride bulls better than the athletes from Crete?”

“I’m the best at my school,” Josh boasted. He *was* a good athlete—but for basketball and football.

Icarus handed some gold coins to the bull riders. They agreed to let the twins enter the contest.

The trumpet sounded again.

“The youngest bull riders go first,” said Icarus. “That’s you. And that’s your bull.” He pointed to the big bull in the pen.

“Oh, great,” said Jess. They wanted Josh to ride the ugly monster bull!

The huge bull was led into the courtyard. He was stomping his feet and kicking up dust.

Josh handed his leather bag to Icarus.

“Take care of this for me?” he asked. The time-compass and journal were inside.

Josh and Jess took their position at the gate.

Jess took a last look at the painting of the young bull rider on the Wizard. She had to face the bull and wave her hands, then move aside quickly.

"Be careful, Jess," said Josh. He stepped behind her.

Jess nodded. "I can do this, I can do this . . . ," she said to herself over and over.

The crowd was excited. Everyone was yelling and shouting.

Suddenly, the bull was released.

"Go!" shouted Josh. "Go now!"

Jess took a deep breath. She dashed toward the bull, waving her hands wildly.

The crowd cheered when they saw Jess.

The bull moved toward her. His head was down.

Jess turned and ran back. The bull raced behind her.

Josh rushed past her. It was his turn now.

"Hurry!" Jess shouted. The bull turned his big head and looked directly at Josh.

The crowd was shouting for Josh to make a move.

"Steady," Josh said to himself. He dashed into the courtyard and ran.

The bull started to gallop toward Josh. The animal's head was down. His horns were straight up.

Josh leaned forward and raised his arms. He ran toward the galloping bull.

Clouds of dust filled the air. The crowd cheered wildly.

Josh grabbed the bull's horns and tossed himself up. Next Josh pushed off with his hands and leaped backward. In one motion, he somersaulted over the bull's back.

Josh landed on his feet.

The spectators were cheering. They were going wild!

Jess ran toward her brother. They jumped up and down and hugged each other.

"We did it! We did it!" Jess screamed.

The palace guards rushed over to Jess and Josh. They formed a circle around them.

"Come with us, strangers," said the tallest guard. "The king wants to meet you."

Jess and Josh followed the guards.

Icarus moved through the crowd. He waited at the bottom of the platform.

The guards pushed Jess and Josh with their spears. Slowly, they stepped up onto the golden platform. They stood in front of King Minos.

"Well, well. Who are my new champions?" asked the king. He rubbed his chin and stared at Jess and Josh.

The king looked closely. Had he seen a face like Josh's before?

Josh stepped before the king.

"My name is Josh. This is my sister, Jess," he said. "We're looking for our uncle."

"Can you help us find Uncle Harry?" Jess asked boldly. She tried to be brave.

Now the king looked angry. He knew that name.

"Ah-ri," he said. "Yes, I know this Ah-ri. *The thief!*"

The guards stepped forward and raised their spears.

"Take them away," the king said angrily.

The guards grabbed Josh and Jess and rushed them off the platform.

"Oh, man," Josh said. "They think we're thieves, too."

Icarus was at the bottom of the steps. He was pointing to Josh's leather bag and holding it up.

Josh shook his head. He didn't want his friend to get into trouble.

Icarus pointed to the sky. Then he disappeared into the crowd.

The tall guard was laughing now. He gripped Jess's arm tightly.

"What's so funny?" asked Jess. She tried to kick the guard.

"You're going to see your uncle Ah-ri all right," said the guard. "Just in time for dinner!"

Chapter 8

In the Labyrinth

The sun was still high in the sky when they got to the labyrinth. It was quiet.

The guards marched Jess and Josh to the entrance of the giant maze. They took the path to the left. The walls on both sides of the labyrinth were at least seven feet high. The winding passageway through the maze was narrow and dark.

"In here," said the guards. They opened a wooden door to a small room.

The tall guard pushed Josh and Jess into the guardhouse.

"Hey," said Josh. "Watch out!" Jess checked her robe. The Wizard was safe in her pocket.

The guards bolted the door and left.

Josh and Jess looked around. A small window near the roof let in some light. They heard a soft moaning sound across the room. They weren't alone.

Josh pointed to a shape in the dark corner.

Jess rushed over and saw that it was a man. He was tied up. Long hair covered his face, but there was no mistaking who it was.

"Uncle Harry! Uncle Harry! Are you okay?" asked Jess, untying him. Josh untied the last knot.

The man opened his eyes. Uncle Harry looked up at the twins. They were four years older now, but their faces were familiar.

Uncle Harry gave Jess and Josh a big hug.

"You kids are awesome!" he said. "But what are you doing here?"

"We found your journal and the time-compass in the trunk," said Josh.

"And the piece of stone with picture writing," said Jess.

"Pretty clever, you two," Uncle Harry said. "You figured out how to set the time-travel device. You're brave to come and rescue me."

Josh and Jess looked at each other.

They remembered the contest. And the charging bull.

"Yeah," said Jess. "Getting here was the easy part!"

"Uncle Harry," said Josh. "It's about your leather bag. And the time-compass and journal . . ."

"We don't have them with us," said Jess. "A friend is keeping them safe for us."

Uncle Harry stood up slowly. He found his hat and shook the dust from his clothes. "We're going to need those things to get you home."

Josh wanted to know more about the time-compass.

The trunk in the attic held objects from

long ago. Where had they come from? Who did they belong to?

"You're not a thief, are you, Uncle Harry?" Jess asked.

Uncle Harry shook his head. He tied his long hair back into a ponytail. Then he put on the leather hat.

"No, I'm not," he said. "Four years ago, I found the time-travel device—the time-compass—in the ruins of an ancient Greek temple. It was buried with sacred objects."

"Stuff like the piece of stone with the picture writing?" asked Josh.

"Yes," Uncle Harry said. "I bring ancient treasures back in time to where they belong. To their true owners."

Just then, they heard a low rumbling in the distance. Uncle Harry stopped talking and listened.

"I'll tell you all about it later. Right now we have to get out of here," he said. "And fast!"

They heard another rumble. It sounded like a wounded animal.

The Minotaur was waking up from his afternoon nap.

The monster was hungry.

"Wow!" said Josh. "Is the Minotaur for real, Uncle Harry?"

"He's real, all right. And he's ready for his dinner," said their uncle. There wasn't much time before the guards returned.

Josh remembered something. He picked up a stick and started to draw on the dirt floor.

Uncle Harry bent down. He looked closely at Josh's drawing. It was the plan of the labyrinth.

"Here." Josh marked the secret gate. "This is where we can escape the maze."

"Awesome!" said Uncle Harry.

"Our friend Icarus showed us," said Jess. "His father designed the labyrinth."

She pulled the Wizard from her pocket. She

searched for *labyrinth* and *Minotaur,* then read aloud:

"I wish Theseus were here now," said Jess.

Uncle Harry stared at the screen. He looked back at the drawing in the dirt.

"I think we can do this," said Uncle Harry. "We're here," he said, pointing to Josh's drawing. "The secret gate isn't far."

They heard another roar. This time it was louder.

The Minotaur was hungry–and moving their way!

"Time to get out of here!" said Uncle Harry. He looked up at the small window.

"Josh," he said, "I can lift you up to that window."

Uncle Harry cupped his hands. Josh took a step and jumped. He reached the window and pulled himself up. The opening was small, but he squeezed through. Josh jumped down on the other side. He lifted the heavy bolt and opened the door.

They rushed out and looked around. High stone walls were on each side. They were in the middle of the labyrinth.

"Where to now?" asked Jess.

"That way!" said Uncle Harry, pointing to the path on the left.

They heard another roar.

"Hurry!" said Jess. The monster was closer.

"This is one time I want to skip dinner!" Josh shouted.

He ran after Jess and Uncle Harry into the maze.

Chapter 9

Escape

The Minotaur was moving slowly.

The beast followed the winding dirt paths. He was looking for his dinner.

A slight breeze was blowing through the labyrinth. The Minotaur stopped to sniff the air. He roared when he smelled the scent of his victims.

"Did you hear *that*?" Jess whispered to Josh.

Josh nodded. He took a deep breath. The Minotaur wasn't far away.

"Stay close behind me," said Uncle Harry. "We're almost there."

They crept through the maze. They tried not to make noise. The path was narrow

and dark. The secret gate was ahead.

"Over here," said Uncle Harry. He led them to a break in the stone wall.

Jess and Josh looked up. In the shadows, they saw a small opening. Just in time, they ducked into the hidden passageway. From the other direction, the guards were coming around the corner.

"Wait," Uncle Harry whispered, waving to Jess and Josh to stay down. They hid in the shadows.

Two palace guards hurried past them. Their

spears were pointed at a young man. He was dressed in a white tunic with a wide leather belt. A gold band held back his short curly hair.

"From his clothing, I'd say that prisoner is from Athens," said Uncle Harry.

Jess raised her head and peeked out. "Do you think that's Theseus?"

"That could be him," said Uncle Harry. "Maybe you got your wish, Jess."

Jess nodded. She showed Josh the Book Wizard. The king of Athens had sent Theseus to kill the Minotaur.

"I bet he escapes," Josh whispered. "He'll see the drawing of the maze on the dirt floor."

"Yay! Theseus will take care of that Minotaur!" Jess said, pumping her fist in the air. "Take that, you ugly beast!"

Uncle Harry waved to Jess and Josh to follow him.

Suddenly, the path split in two. They stopped. Uncle Harry opened the journal and checked the map of the labyrinth.

He chose the passageway to the right. They rushed down the path.

Ahead was an open space surrounded by olive trees. A hill sloped down toward the city.

They were out of the labyrinth.

Outside the wind was blowing hard. The olive trees twisted in the breeze.

"Hey," said Jess, covering her eyes. "What's happening? I can't see anything."

"Close your eyes," shouted Uncle Harry.

"Josh, hold on to your sister. Stay down until the dust storm blows over."

Uncle Harry knelt on the ground. He put his arms around Josh and Jess. He held them close.

After a few minutes, the worst of the storm was over.

Their heads were still down when they heard the flapping of wings. A giant shadow fell over them.

Josh was the first to look up.

"Wow!" he cried out. "Look at that!" Something was coming from behind the clouds.

Jess opened her eyes and stared at the figure in the sky. She couldn't believe her eyes.

Icarus was flying above them!

He was wearing giant wings made of feathers and wax on a wooden frame. Leather straps held his arms to the mechanical wings.

A familiar leather bag was wrapped around Icarus's waist. A second pair of wings was tied to his legs.

"Icarus! Icarus!" shouted Josh, waving his arms. "Down here!"

Josh ran ahead to meet their friend.

Uncle Harry laughed. He turned to Jess.

"Don't you know?" he asked. "Your friend is famous."

Jess turned on the Wizard and typed in I-C-A-R-U-S and W-I-N-G-S. She read aloud:

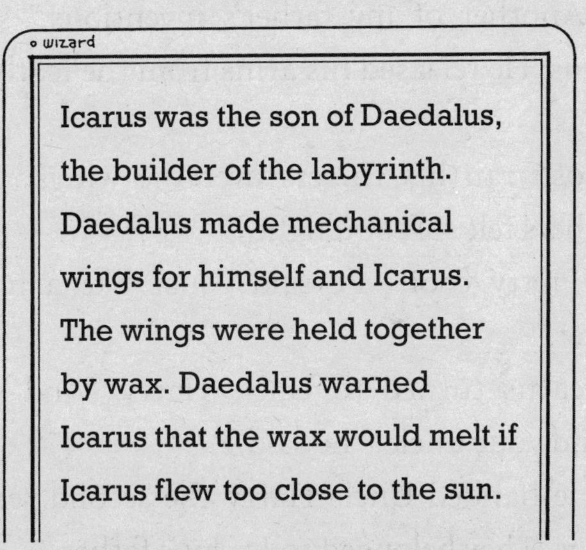

Jess looked up and waved to her friend.

Uncle Harry guided Icarus to the ground.

Icarus spread his giant wings and swooped down. He landed in a small cloud of dust.

"Oh, man," said Josh. "Are we happy to see you!"

Jess ran over. She had a big smile on her face.

"You came back, Icarus!" she said. "And you can fly!"

"Another of my father's inventions," said Icarus. He released his arms from the feathery wings.

Josh ran his fingers over the wings. The feathers felt soft and light.

"Pretty cool!" he said. "Just like a hang glider."

Icarus turned to Uncle Harry. "And you found your uncle!" he said.

He handed Uncle Harry the second set of wings. They belonged to Icarus's father.

Uncle Harry put his arms through the frames and flapped the wings.

"Awesome," said Uncle Harry. "These work for me."

Icarus looked up at the afternoon sky. He attached the wings to his arms again. "We have to go. It will be dark soon."

Uncle Harry turned and walked toward the hill. He looked down at the city.

"Over here," he called. "I think we can take off from this hill."

He ran back to check the distance. He talked with Icarus, pointing beyond the city.

"Grab my hand, Jess," said Icarus. Uncle Harry held on to Josh.

Jess wasn't sure about all this. She pulled her hand away.

"Trust me," said Icarus. "We can fly together."

Josh turned toward his sister. He held her hand. "Jess, you can do it! Take a deep breath . . . and run!"

"Okay," Jess said quietly. She gave her hand

to Icarus. "But I'm closing my eyes. I don't want to look down!"

They lined up, hand in hand, with Josh and Jess in the middle. Uncle Harry and Icarus were on the ends. They started to flap the giant wings.

"Ready," Uncle Harry called out, "set, go!"

They ran together toward the side of the hill.

Uncle Harry and Icarus moved the wings up and down, faster and faster. Their feet left the ground. The wind was lifting them higher and higher.

They were flying!

Chapter 10

Fly Away

The sky was blue. The sun was near the horizon. Soon it would be sunset.

Jess and Josh held on tightly to Icarus and Uncle Harry.

The giant mechanical wings were flapping in the wind. Up they went, soaring above the clouds.

Jess felt the breeze on her face. Slowly, she opened her eyes.

"Wow!" She looked at the ground below. Maybe this was all a dream!

"Are we really flying?" Jess asked, turning to her brother.

Josh was having fun. Flying was better than

bull riding. He was gliding, moving from side to side, sailing on the wind!

"Hey, cut it out!" cried Jess. "Do you want us to fall?"

"This is amazing," Josh said. Where were they now? It didn't matter. Josh was having the time of his life.

They flew over a walled city. Jess recognized the large stone building in the middle.

"There," she said. "That must be the Palace of Knossos." It looked like the plan in the Wizard.

The viewing stands were filled. People were still watching the contests. The bulls looked small and far away.

To the left was the labyrinth. In the afternoon shadows, it was hard to see inside the walls.

"Uncle Harry, can we fly lower?" asked Josh. "Maybe we can see the Minotaur."

Icarus turned to Uncle Harry. Together,

they slowed down their mechanical wings and glided down over the maze.

They saw two figures. The larger one was a giant.

"There's the Minotaur," shouted Uncle Harry. He turned one wing to point below.

"Gross!" said Jess. The monster had the head of a bull and the legs of a man. Was he a big man wearing a mask, or was he really a beast?

The Minotaur wasn't alone. The stranger with the guards was there, too. He held a spear against the Minotaur.

"I bet that's Theseus!" Josh cried out. He must have escaped. So Theseus did fight the Minotaur after all!

"It could be him," said Uncle Harry. "Many people believe the ancient stories."

Icarus turned to Uncle Harry.

"We'd better fly higher and catch the winds," he said. Icarus flapped his wings harder. They soared higher toward the setting sun.

"We can't be too far from the sea," said Uncle Harry.

In a few minutes, they could see blue waters. Wooden boats were in the harbor.

Uncle Harry pointed his left wing to a large boat tied to the dock.

"That's my boat!" he shouted. "Let's start to go down now."

Icarus and Uncle Harry glided downward on a gentle sea breeze. They headed toward the docks, where the boats were tied.

Josh and Jess smelled the salty sea air. Lower and lower, they moved toward the shoreline.

They came to a stop, landing on their feet.

"Whew!" Jess took a deep breath. It felt good to be on the ground again.

Uncle Harry folded the mechanical wings and returned them to Icarus. He took the leather bag from Icarus and hung it on his shoulder. The time-compass was safe inside.

"Thanks, Icarus," said Uncle Harry. "That ride was awesome."

Icarus turned to Jess.

"Are you okay?" he asked. "You are very brave. I won't forget you."

Jess gave Icarus a big smile. She remembered something important from the Wizard.

"Wait! The wax on your wings can melt. Don't fly too close to the sun," she warned Icarus.

Icarus laughed. "You sound like my father!" He gave Jess a big hug.

Josh shook his hand. They were going to miss their new friend.

It was time to leave. Icarus turned and ran along the shoreline. A strong sea breeze lifted him. He flapped his mechanical wings and took off.

Icarus soared higher and higher into the setting sun.

Chapter 11

The Secret of the Tablet

Jess and Josh watched as Icarus disappeared behind the clouds.

"Thank you, Icarus." Jess waved a last good-bye.

"Come on," said Josh. They raced toward the harbor.

No one was around. Several boats were tied to the dock. Waves were splashing against the sides. The boats were moving back and forth in the wind.

"Where's Uncle Harry?" asked Jess. No more

running from monsters! No more flying! It was time to go home.

"Look!" Josh pointed.

Uncle Harry was on the deck of the largest boat. He was on his knees, opening a wooden box. It was partly hidden below the sails.

Josh and Jess ran to the dock. They watched as Uncle Harry took a large sack from the box. He carefully placed it on the dock. It looked heavy.

"What's in the sack?" whispered Jess. "Is it gold and silver treasure from the palace?"

Josh shook his head. "You heard what Uncle Harry said. He's not a thief."

Jess wasn't sure. Maybe King Minos was right. They didn't know their uncle well.

Uncle Harry jumped onto the dock. He opened the sack. Gently, he took out a large stone tablet.

Josh and Jess walked over.

"What's that?" Josh asked, pointing to the stone tablet.

"Did you steal treasures from King Minos?" asked Jess.

Uncle Harry laughed. He laid the stone tablet on the dock.

"No, I'm not a thief," he said, shaking his head. "I came to Knossos for something far more important than gold and silver."

"Tell us why you're here," said Josh. "You never finished your story."

"And how are we going to get home?" asked Jess.

Uncle Harry dug into his leather bag and pulled out the journal.

"Here's a clue," he said. He found the drawing of the tablet with the missing piece.

Jess and Josh stared at the large stone tablet at Uncle Harry's feet. They looked at the drawing in the journal. It was the same tablet.

“I hid the tablet on the boat before the guards found me,” said Uncle Harry.

“There’s more.” He reached into the leather bag. He put the stone piece with the picture writing next to the stone tablet. Then the time-compass.

“But why did you travel through time to come *here*?” asked Jess. “To Crete?”

Uncle Harry pointed to a row of picture writing on the broken piece. “These marks led me to Crete. This stone was buried with the time-compass in an ancient temple in Greece. But the tablet was missing."

Josh held the small stone piece. "Where did you find the tablet?"

"King Minos stole it from Athens long ago," said Uncle Harry. "I traveled through time to get it back. Now I have to return the tablet. To the temple where it belongs."

Uncle Harry stood up and gathered his things. Josh handed back the broken piece.

Jess and Josh were glad. Uncle Harry wasn't a thief after all. He was returning the tablet to its real owner.

"I studied the picture writing for a long time," said Uncle Harry. "It tells me where to go next. And I have more sacred objects to return."

Josh looked closely at the strange writing. It was a puzzle. A really old one.

"Are you collecting clues?" asked Jess. "Is that why you left your things in the trunk?"

Uncle Harry nodded. "Yes, to keep them safe. I didn't mean for you and Josh to follow me."

"Yeah," said Josh. "The time-compass sent us here. To Crete."

"And we rescued you, don't forget!" Jess said. "You needed our help."

Uncle Harry smiled at the twins. "You two were awesome! And we were lucky you weren't hurt."

He took a quick look at his journal. Then he handed it to Josh.

"Keep this safe in the trunk in the attic. Don't show it to anyone. Promise?" asked Uncle Harry.

"Yes, I promise," Josh said, taking the journal.

"Jess?" said Uncle Harry. "What about you?"

"Okay, I guess," Jess agreed.

But she wasn't sure. Maybe they should tell Mom and Dad. "Will you go to Athens now, Uncle Harry?"

"Can we go with you to return the tablet?" asked Josh. He was ready for another adventure.

"No way," said Jess. She stared at her brother. Was Josh nuts?

Uncle Harry laughed. "Josh, I think you're an explorer, like me."

"Please, Uncle Harry," said Josh.

"I'll send for you when I need help, how about that?" said Uncle Harry. "But not this time. It's too dangerous. I'm sending you home right now."

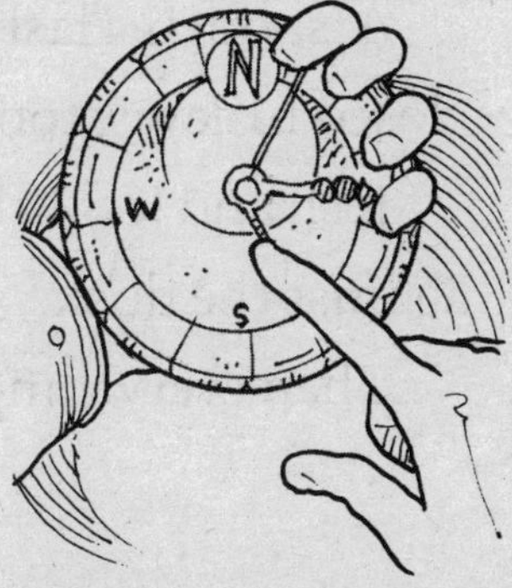

Uncle Harry moved the hands of the time-compass. He set the time and the direction. Then he pressed a switch on the side. The time-compass started to make clicking sounds.

Uncle Harry turned to Jess and Josh.

"Are you ready?"

"Wait, Uncle Harry!" shouted Josh. "Where are you going next? How can we find you?"

The time-compass was clicking loudly now.

They took a last look at their uncle.

"Awesome," said Uncle Harry. He waved good-bye.

Jess closed her eyes and grabbed Josh's hand.

"Good-bye," said Josh.

"Bye, Uncle Harry," said Jess.

A sudden flash of light blinded Josh. He closed his eyes, too.

Josh and Jess listened to the waves splashing against the dock.

Then everything was quiet.

Chapter 12

Home Again

Jess was the first to open her eyes.

She looked around. They were back in the attic in the big white house.

Josh was holding her hand. Uncle Harry's journal was in his other hand.

"We're home," Josh said. The trunk with all the stickers was next to the window.

Jess let go of Josh's hand. She rushed over to the window and peeked out.

"Yeah, we're here, all right," said Jess. It was starting to get dark. The sidewalk was empty. A dog was barking down the street.

It was about the same time as when they had left.

"Did we just travel in time," Josh asked, "or was I dreaming?"

Jess shook her head. "That was no dream," she said. "But it was magic!"

She looked down. Her sandals and white robe were gone. She reached into the pocket of her sweatshirt. The Wizard was still there.

"Hey," said Josh. "What happened to my Greek clothes?" He was wearing jeans and sneakers again.

"Were we really in ancient Crete with Uncle Harry?" asked Jess.

It was hard to believe that they had traveled through time.

"Did we really enter the bull-riding contest? Did we rescue Uncle Harry from the labyrinth?" asked Jess.

"It was real, all right," said Josh, holding up the journal. "Don't you remember flying with Icarus and Uncle Harry?" he asked. "It was amazing!"

"I remember," said Jess softly. She wasn't going to forget her friend. Or Uncle Harry.

"But who's going to believe us?" she wondered, shaking her head.

Josh opened the journal. He flipped through the pages. He found the drawing of the stone tablet. It was all there.

He remembered their promise to Uncle Harry.

"Jess, we can't tell anyone," said Josh.

"Not even Mom and Dad?" asked Jess. She didn't like to keep secrets.

Josh shook his head. "We can't tell anyone. We gave our word. A promise is a promise."

He walked over to the old trunk.

"We'd better put the journal back where we got it," said Josh.

Jess turned away from the window. She thought about the big ugly bull in the contest. She wasn't afraid of any squirrels now!

She started to close the trunk, then stopped.

"Wait," said Jess. "What other clues are in the journal?"

Josh looked at his sister. Jess looked different, not like the old Jess. She looked excited, like the girl in the bull ring.

"Who's the brave one now?" Josh laughed. "Are you ready for a new adventure so soon?"

"I just want to know, that's all. Where's Uncle Harry going next?" she asked. "He might need our help."

Josh sat on the floor next to the old trunk. He opened the journal and found the pages about Crete. He turned the page.

"What does the journal say?" asked Jess. She sat next to Josh.

Jess turned on the flashlight. The beam lit up a drawing of a map.

"It looks like a map of ancient Egypt," said

Josh. "See this river here?" he said, pointing to a long wavy line.

Jess moved closer.

"It's marked 'the Nile River,'" she said. "There are other marks for pyramids. They're in the desert."

Josh turned the pages.

"Look," he said. "There's more picture writing."

With the flashlight, Jess searched the old trunk.

There were no more clues.

"We'll have to wait until Uncle Harry needs us. Like the last time," Jess said.

Josh put the journal back into the trunk.

"He'll leave us the time-compass," said Jess. "And a clue, like the piece of stone from the tablet."

"Wow, ancient Egypt!" said Josh.

He couldn't wait for their next adventure.

"Jessica! Joshua! Dinnertime!" came a voice from downstairs.

It was their mother calling. Time to leave the attic.

Josh closed the lid on the old trunk.

"We're coming!" shouted Jess.

They took off and headed down the stairs.